DUDLEY PUBLIC LIBRARIES

The loan of this book may be renewed if not required by other readers, by contacting the library from which it was borrowed.

Note to parents, carers and teachers

Read it yourself is a series of modern stories, favourite characters and traditional tales written in a simple way for children who are learning to read. The books can be read independently or as part of a guided reading session.

Each book is carefully structured to include many high-frequency words vital for first reading. The sentences on each page are supported closely by pictures to help with understanding, and to offer lively details to talk about.

The books are graded into four levels that progressively introduce wider vocabulary and longer stories as a reader's ability and confidence grows.

Ideas for use

• Although your child will now be progressing towards silent, independent reading, let her know that your help and encouragement is always available.

• Developing readers can be concentrating so hard on the words that they sometimes don't fully grasp the meaning of what they're reading. Answering the puzzle questions at the end of the book will help with understanding.

For more information and advice on Read it yourself and book banding, visit **www.ladybird.com/readityourself**

Book
Band
9

Level 4 is ideal for children who are ready to read longer stories with a wider vocabulary and are eager to start reading independently.

Special features:

Clear type

Full, exciting story

Richer, more varied vocabulary

"Stay in the garden, Peter," said Grandfather. "Never go into the meadow on your own."

"But why not?" said Peter.

"There is a hungry wolf in the dark forest," said Grandfather. He could come creeping into the meadow and eat you up!"

8

9

Longer sentences

Detailed illustrations capture the imagination

"Come back at once, Peter!" said Grandfather.

So Peter climbed over the wall and went back into the garden with his grandfather.

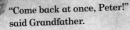

22

23

Educational Consultant: Geraldine Taylor
Book Banding Consultant: Kate Ruttle

LADYBIRD BOOKS

UK | USA | Canada | Ireland | Australia
India | New Zealand | South Africa

Ladybird Books is part of the Penguin Random House group of companies
whose addresses can be found at global.penguinrandomhouse.com.

ladybird.com

 Penguin
Random House
UK

First published 2015
001

Peter
and the Wolf

Illustrated by Milly Teggle

Peter and his grandfather lived next to a beautiful meadow.

Next to the meadow, there was a dark forest. And in the middle of the forest, there lived a hungry wolf.

"Stay in the garden, Peter," said Grandfather. "Never go into the meadow on your own."

"But why not?" said Peter.

"There is a hungry wolf in the dark forest," said Grandfather. "He could come creeping into the meadow and eat you up!"

Peter looked over the garden wall. The meadow looked very beautiful.

A little red bird flew up to a big tree. "Peter!" called the bird. "Why don't you come and play in the meadow?"

Peter climbed over the garden wall and went into the meadow.

There was a pond in the middle of the meadow.

A duck waddled past Peter, then she jumped into the pond and swam away.

The little red bird flew down
to the duck.

"Come back!" she said to the duck.
"What a funny walk! Why don't
you fly like me?"

"I don't want to fly like you," said
the duck. "Why don't you swim
like me?"

The two birds were very cross
with one another, and they made
a lot of noise.

Suddenly, Peter saw a cat come
creeping towards the birds.
"Look out!" called Peter. "The cat
will catch you!"

At once, the little red bird flew up to the top of the big tree and the duck swam to the middle of the pond.

Just then, Peter's grandfather came into the garden.

He looked over the wall and saw Peter in the meadow. He was very cross with him.

"Come back at once, Peter!" said Grandfather.

So Peter climbed over the wall and went back into the garden with his grandfather.

Suddenly, the wolf came creeping out of the forest.

He saw the little red bird, the duck and the cat. He was so hungry that he wanted to eat them all.

The cat climbed to the very top of the tree, where the little red bird was sitting.

The two of them waited to see what would happen next.

The frightened duck jumped
out of the pond! She waddled
off as fast as she could. But the
hungry wolf ran faster and caught
her in his big mouth!

Then the wolf walked round and round the tree where the cat and the little red bird were sitting.

The hungry wolf looked up at them. They were very frightened.

Peter found a very long rope
and climbed on top of the
garden wall.

"Fly around the wolf's head!"
he called out to the
little red bird.
"Make him dizzy!
But stay away from
his big mouth!"

The little red bird flew round and round the wolf's head. The hungry wolf tried to catch the little red bird, but after a time he was very dizzy.

Peter climbed up the big tree.
Then he let the rope down and
caught the wolf by the tail.
The wolf jumped up and down
and tried to get away.
But Peter held on to the rope.

Just then, Grandfather saw Peter sitting in the tree.

"What are you doing up there?" he called.

"I've got the wolf by the tail," said Peter. "Look!"

Suddenly, hunters came into
the meadow, looking for the wolf.

"Here he is," said Peter.
"Take him away!"

The hunters took the wolf
to another forest, a very
long way away from Peter
and his grandfather, the cat,
and the little red bird.

So Peter's grandfather then let him play in the beautiful meadow, with the little red bird and the cat.

How much do you remember about the story of Peter and the Wolf? Answer these questions and find out!

- Who does Peter live with?

- Who lives in the dark forest?

- What is in the middle of the meadow?

- What does Peter say the cat will do to the birds?

- How does Peter catch the wolf?

- Who takes the wolf away?

Unjumble these words to make words from the story, then match them to the correct pictures.

letlit der rbdi   ckdu   Gnatherdfar

Preet   tac   lofw

Tick the books you've read!

Level 3

Level 4